D1470470

BLACK PANTHER

A NATION UNDER OUR FEET: PART 7

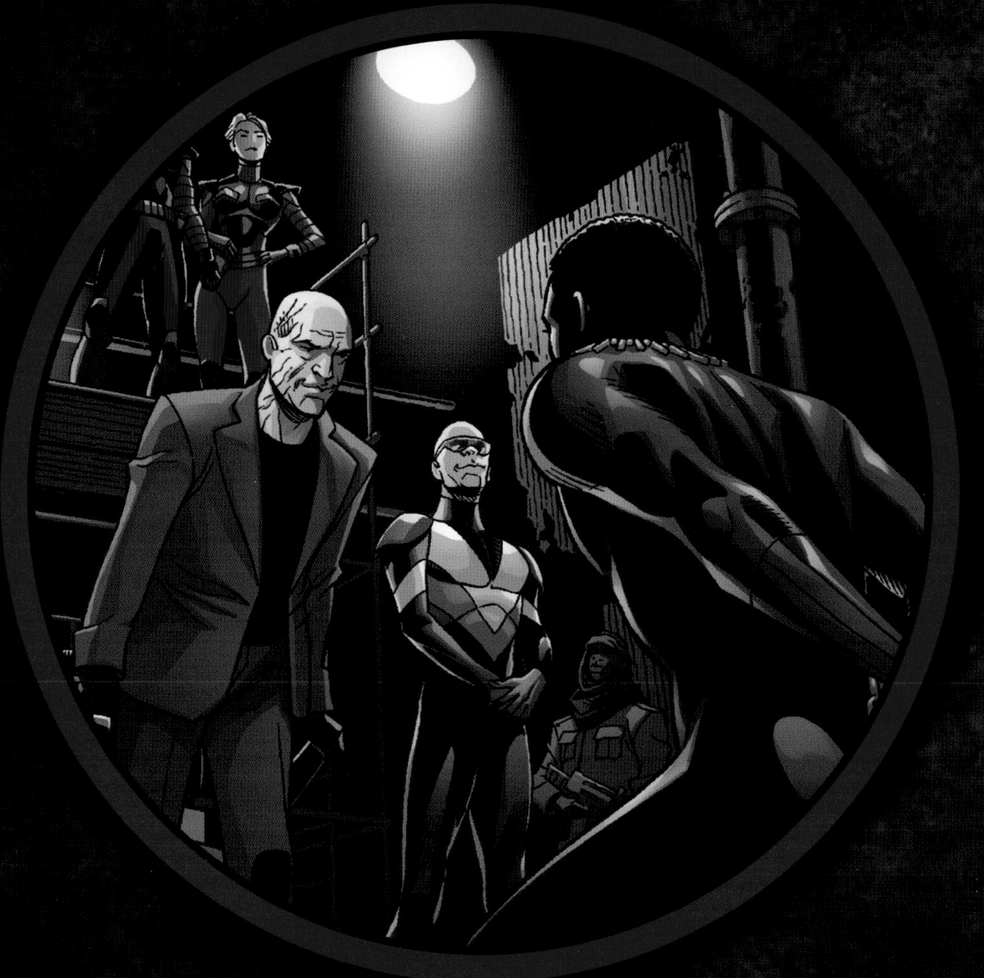

MARVEL

ABDO
Spotlight

ABDOBOOKS.COM

Reinforced library bound edition published in 2021 by Spotlight,
a division of ABDO, PO Box 398166, Minneapolis, Minnesota 55439.
Spotlight produces high-quality reinforced library bound editions for
schools and libraries. Published by agreement with Marvel Characters, Inc.

Printed in the United States of America, North Mankato, Minnesota.
092020
012021

THIS BOOK CONTAINS
RECYCLED MATERIALS

Library of Congress Control Number: 2020942382

Publisher's Cataloging-in-Publication Data

Names: Coates, Ta-Nehisi, author. | Sprouse, Chris; Story, Karl; Martin, Laura; Wong,
    Walden; Stelfreeze, Brian; Hanna, Scott, illustrators.
Title: A nation under our feet / by Ta-Nehisi Coates; illustrated by Chris Sprouse,
    Karl Story, Laura Martin, Walden Wong, Brian Stelfreeze and Scott Hanna.
Description: Minneapolis, Minnesota: Spotlight, 2021 | Series: Black panther
Summary: With a dramatic upheaval in Wakanda on the horizon, T'Challa knows his
    kingdom needs to change to survive, but he struggles to find balance in his
    roles as king and the Black Panther.
Identifiers: ISBN 9781532147784 (pt. 7, lib. bdg.) | ISBN 9781532147791 (pt. 8, lib.
    bdg.) | ISBN 9781532147807 (pt. 9, lib. bdg.) | ISBN 9781532147814 (pt. 10,
    lib. bdg.) | ISBN 9781532147821 (pt. 11, lib. bdg.) | ISBN 9781532147838 (pt.
    12, lib. bdg.)
Subjects: LCSH: Black Panther (Fictitious character)--Juvenile fiction. | Superheroes--
    Juvenile fiction. | Kings and rulers--Juvenile fiction. | Graphic novels--Juvenile
    fiction. | T'Challa, of Wakanda (Fictitious character)--Juvenile fiction.
Classification: DDC 741.5--dc23

Spotlight

A Division of ABDO
abdobooks.com

BLACK PANTHER

AFTER A TERRORIST BOMBING, **KING T'CHALLA**, A.K.A. THE BLACK PANTHER, BEGAN A RELENTLESS COUNTERATTACK ON HIS MANY ENEMIES.

WAKANDA'S SECRET POLICE, THE **HATUT ZERAZE**, INVADED THE JABARI-LANDS TO TAKE ON THE ROGUE **DORA MILAJE** WHO HAD RECENTLY SEIZED CONTROL OF THAT AREA. ELSEWHERE, T'CHALLA ALLOWED HIMSELF TO BE CAPTURED BY **EZEKIEL STANE**, AN ARMS DEALER WHO HAD BEEN SUPPLYING TECHNOLOGY TO THE REBELS STAGING THE ATTEMPTED COUP OF WAKANDA.

USING BLOOD-BORNE NANITE CAMERA TECHNOLOGY PIONEERED BY DOCTOR DOOM, T'CHALLA BROADCAST STANE'S PACT WITH THE REBEL LEADER **TETU**, UNDERMINING THEIR POLITICAL POSITION WITH THE CITIZENS OF WAKANDA. WITH THE TRUTH REVEALED, T'CHALLA CALLS IN **STORM, LUKE CAGE, MISTY KNIGHT**, AND **MANIFOLD**... A.K.A. **THE CREW**.

MEANWHILE, **SHURI** TRAVELS THE PLANE OF COLLECTIVE WAKANDAN MEMORY KNOWN AS THE DJALIA, TRAINING WITH AND LEARNING FROM A GRIOT IN THE FORM OF HER MOTHER.

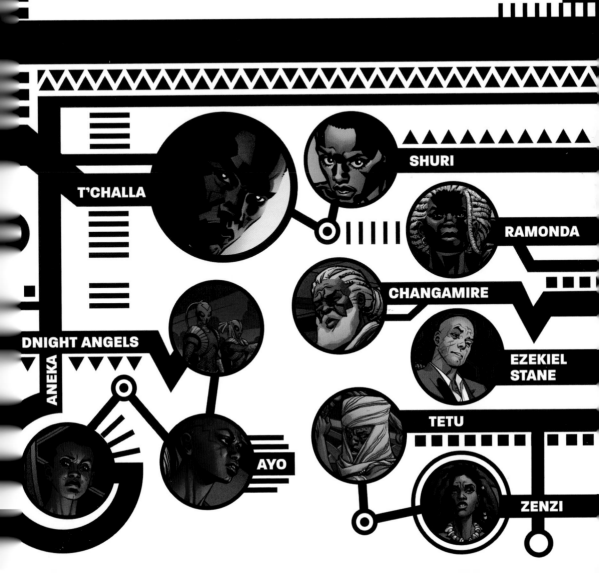

T'CHALLA

SHURI

RAMONDA

CHANGAMIRE

EZEKIEL STANE

DNIGHT ANGELS

ANEKA

AYO

TETU

ZENZI

A NATION UNDER OUR FEET

part 7

writer **TA-NEHISI COATES**

pencils/layouts **CHRIS SPROUSE**

inks/finishes **KARL STORY**   color artist **LAURA**

letterer **VC's JOE SABINO**
design **MANNY MEDEROS**
logo **RIAN HUGHES**
cover by **BRIAN STELFREEZE**
& LAURA MARTIN
variant covers by
MIKE DEODATO & FRANK MARTIN;
ESAD RIBIC; MARGUERITE SAUVAGE;
BILL SIENKIEWICZ; LEINIL YU & JASON KEITH;
SCORPKING COSTUMING with **JUDITH STEPHENS**
assistant editor **CHRIS ROBINSON**
editor **WIL MOSS**
executive editor **TOM BREVOORT**

editor in chief **AXEL ALONSO**   chief creative officer **JOE QUESADA**
publisher **DAN BUCKLEY**   executive producer **ALAN FINE**

BLACK PANTHER   created by
STAN LEE &
JACK KIRBY

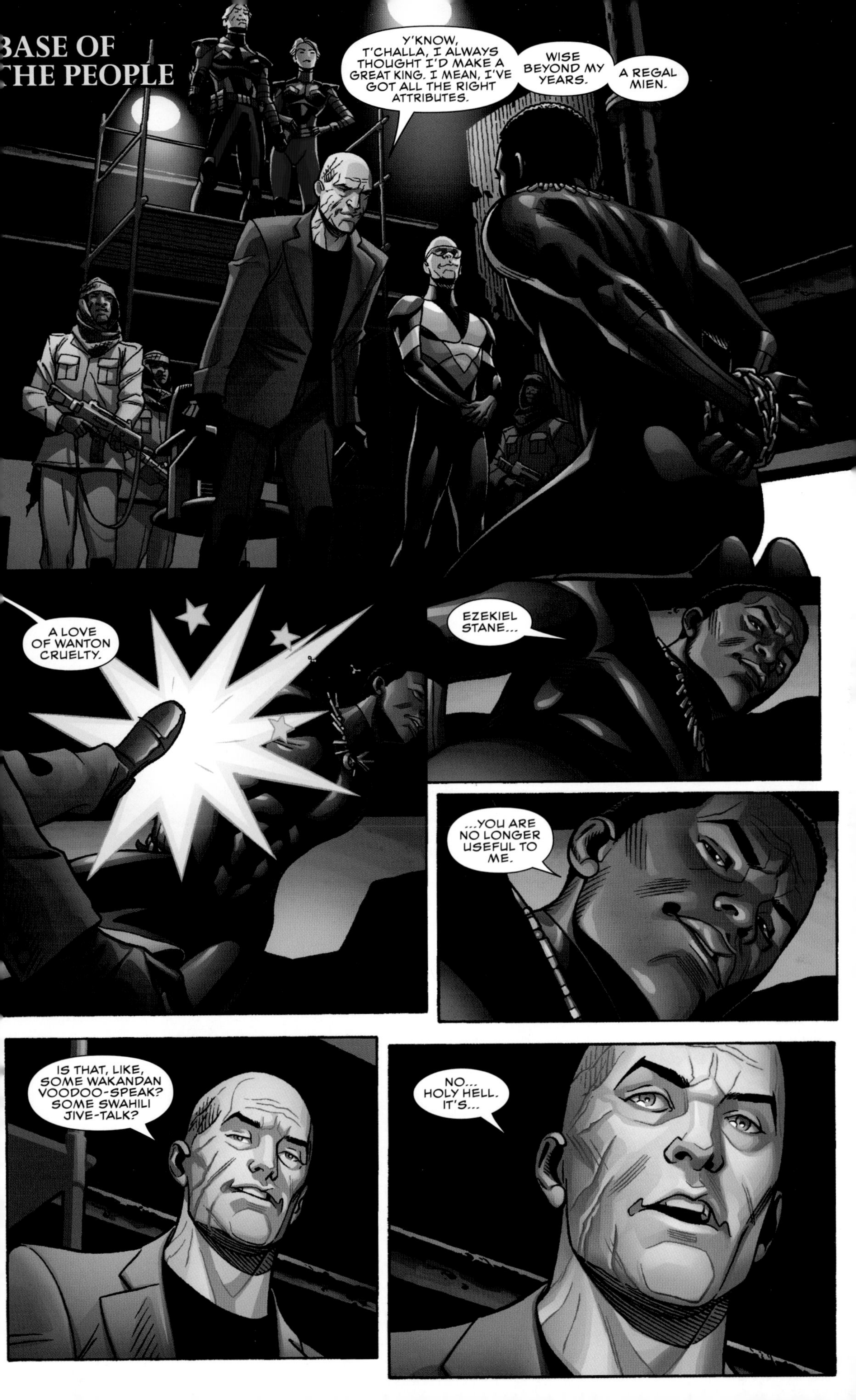
BASE OF
HE PEOPLE
Y'KNOW, T'CHALLA, I ALWAYS THOUGHT I'D MAKE A GREAT KING. I MEAN, I'VE GOT ALL THE RIGHT ATTRIBUTES.
WISE BEYOND MY YEARS.
A REGAL MIEN.
A LOVE OF WANTON CRUELTY.
EZEKIEL STANE...
...YOU ARE NO LONGER USEFUL TO ME.
IS THAT, LIKE, SOME WAKANDAN VOODOO-SPEAK? SOME SWAHILI JIVE-TALK?
NO... HOLY HELL. IT'S...

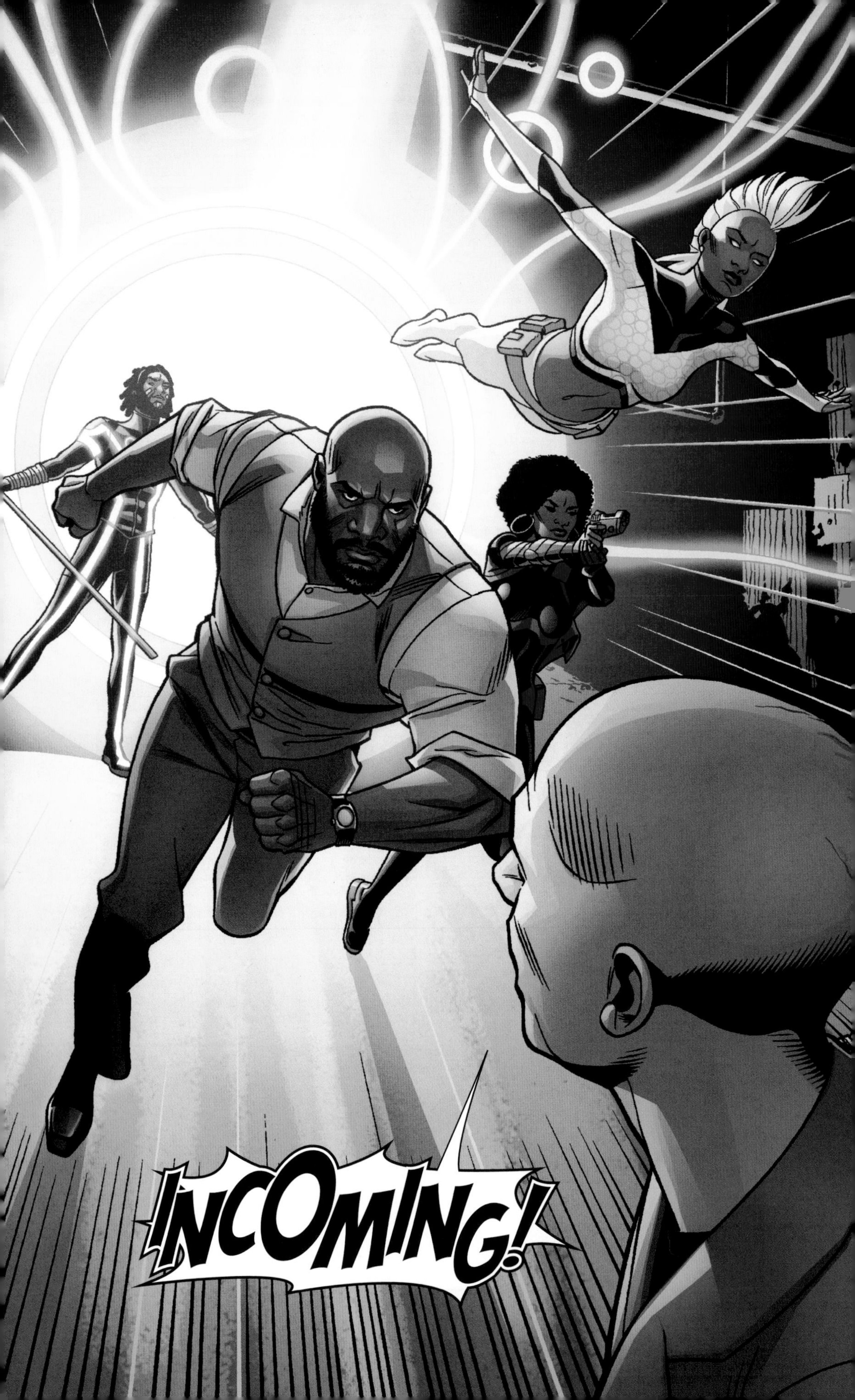
INCOMING!

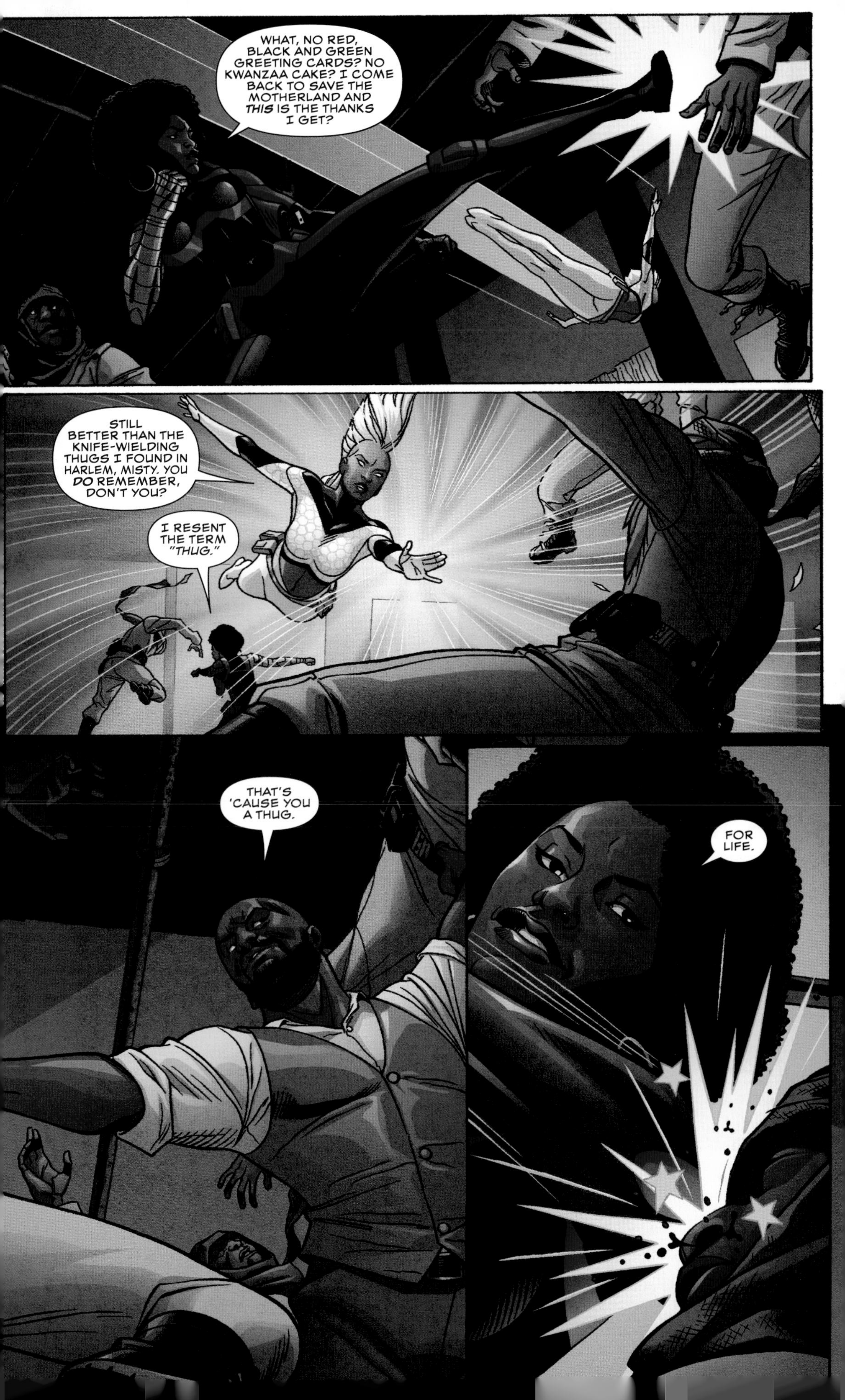
WHAT, NO RED, BLACK AND GREEN GREETING CARDS? NO KWANZAA CAKE? I COME BACK TO SAVE THE MOTHERLAND AND *THIS* IS THE THANKS I GET?
STILL BETTER THAN THE KNIFE-WIELDING THUGS I FOUND IN HARLEM, MISTY. YOU *DO* REMEMBER, DON'T YOU?
I RESENT THE TERM *"THUG."*
THAT'S 'CAUSE YOU A THUG.
FOR LIFE.

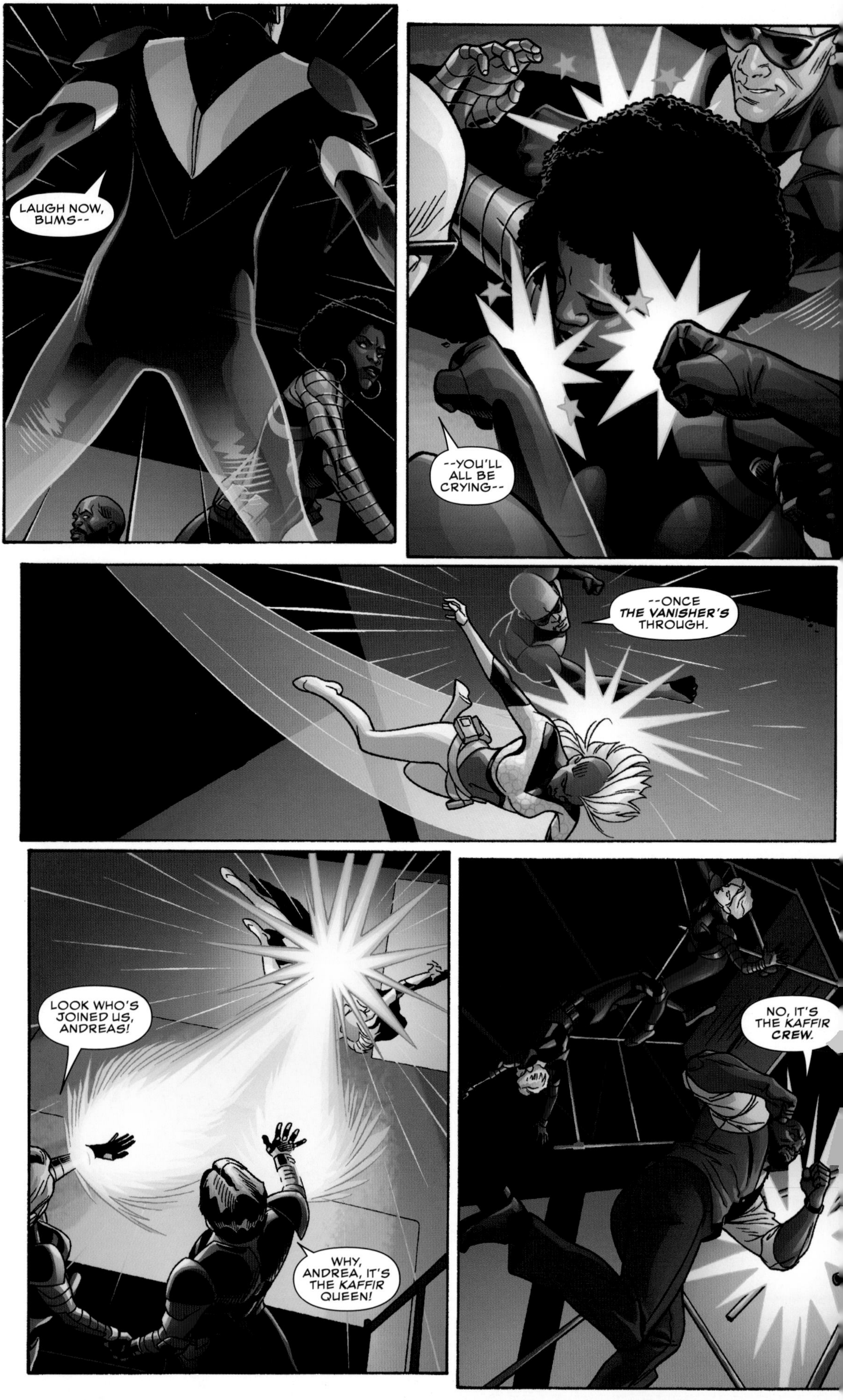
LAUGH NOW, BUMS--
--YOU'LL ALL BE CRYING--
--ONCE *THE VANISHER'S* THROUGH.
LOOK WHO'S JOINED US, ANDREAS!
WHY, ANDREA, IT'S THE *KAFFIR* QUEEN!
NO, IT'S THE *KAFFIR* *CREW.*

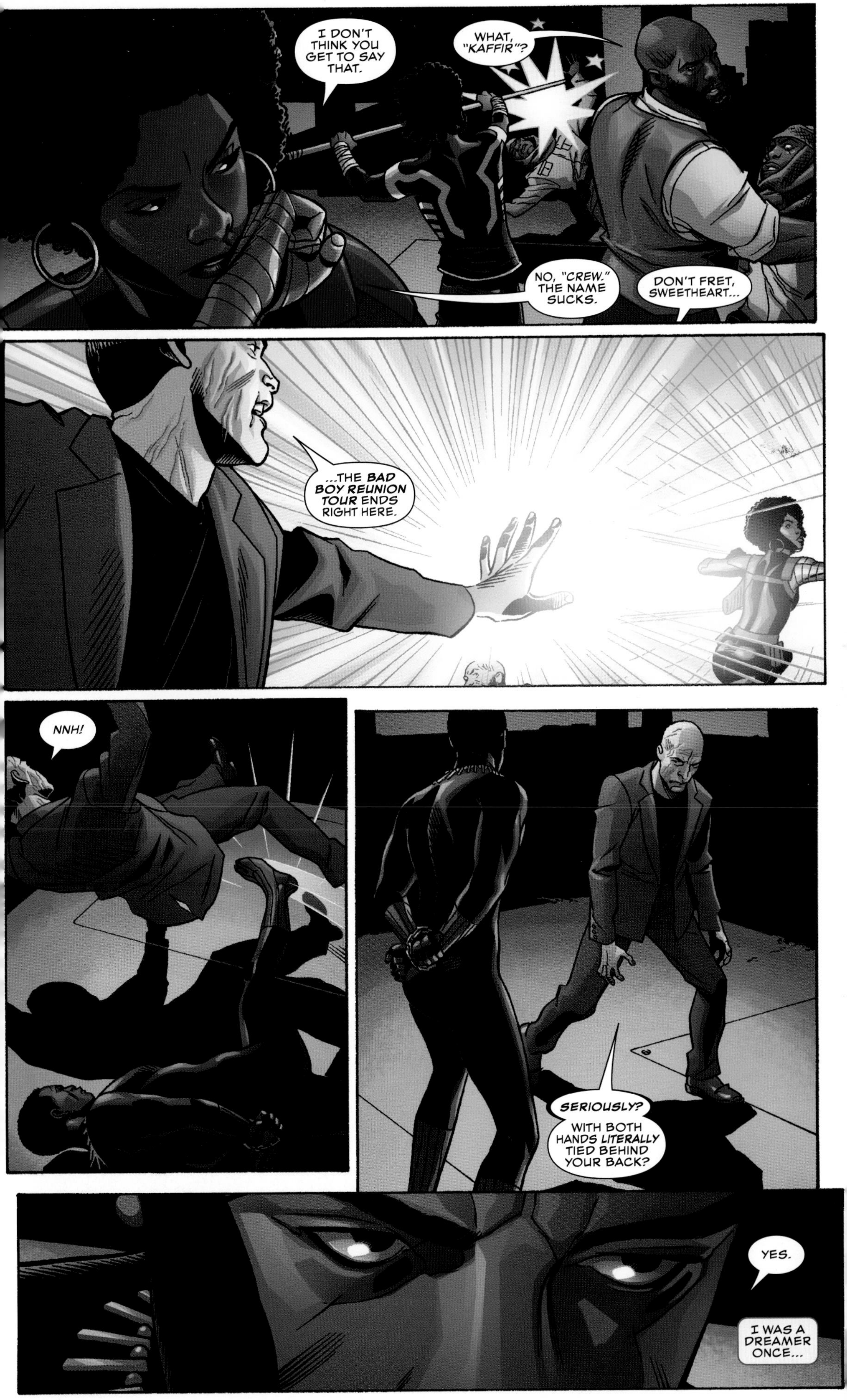
I DON'T THINK YOU GET TO SAY THAT.
WHAT, "*KAFFIR*"?
NO, "*CREW.*" THE NAME SUCKS.
DON'T FRET, SWEETHEART...
...THE ***BAD BOY REUNION TOUR*** ENDS RIGHT HERE.
NNH!
SERIOUSLY?
WITH BOTH HANDS ***LITERALLY*** TIED BEHIND YOUR BACK?
YES.
I WAS A DREAMER ONCE...

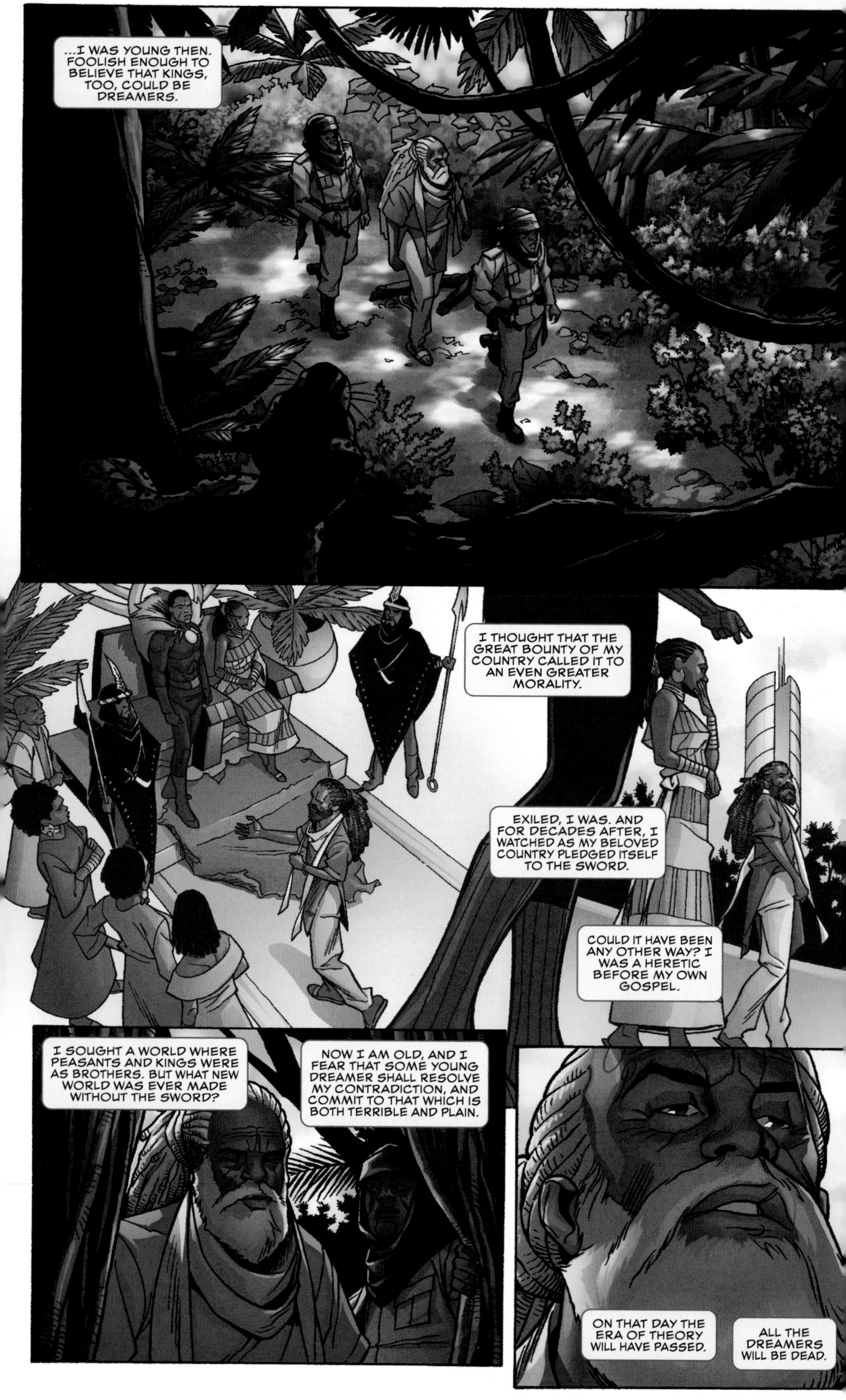
...I WAS YOUNG THEN. FOOLISH ENOUGH TO BELIEVE THAT KINGS, TOO, COULD BE DREAMERS.
I THOUGHT THAT THE GREAT BOUNTY OF MY COUNTRY CALLED IT TO AN EVEN GREATER MORALITY.
EXILED, I WAS. AND FOR DECADES AFTER, I WATCHED AS MY BELOVED COUNTRY PLEDGED ITSELF TO THE SWORD.
COULD IT HAVE BEEN ANY OTHER WAY? I WAS A HERETIC BEFORE MY OWN GOSPEL.
I SOUGHT A WORLD WHERE PEASANTS AND KINGS WERE AS BROTHERS. BUT WHAT NEW WORLD WAS EVER MADE WITHOUT THE SWORD?
NOW I AM OLD, AND I FEAR THAT SOME YOUNG DREAMER SHALL RESOLVE MY CONTRADICTION, AND COMMIT TO THAT WHICH IS BOTH TERRIBLE AND PLAIN.
ON THAT DAY THE ERA OF THEORY WILL HAVE PASSED.
ALL THE DREAMERS WILL BE DEAD.

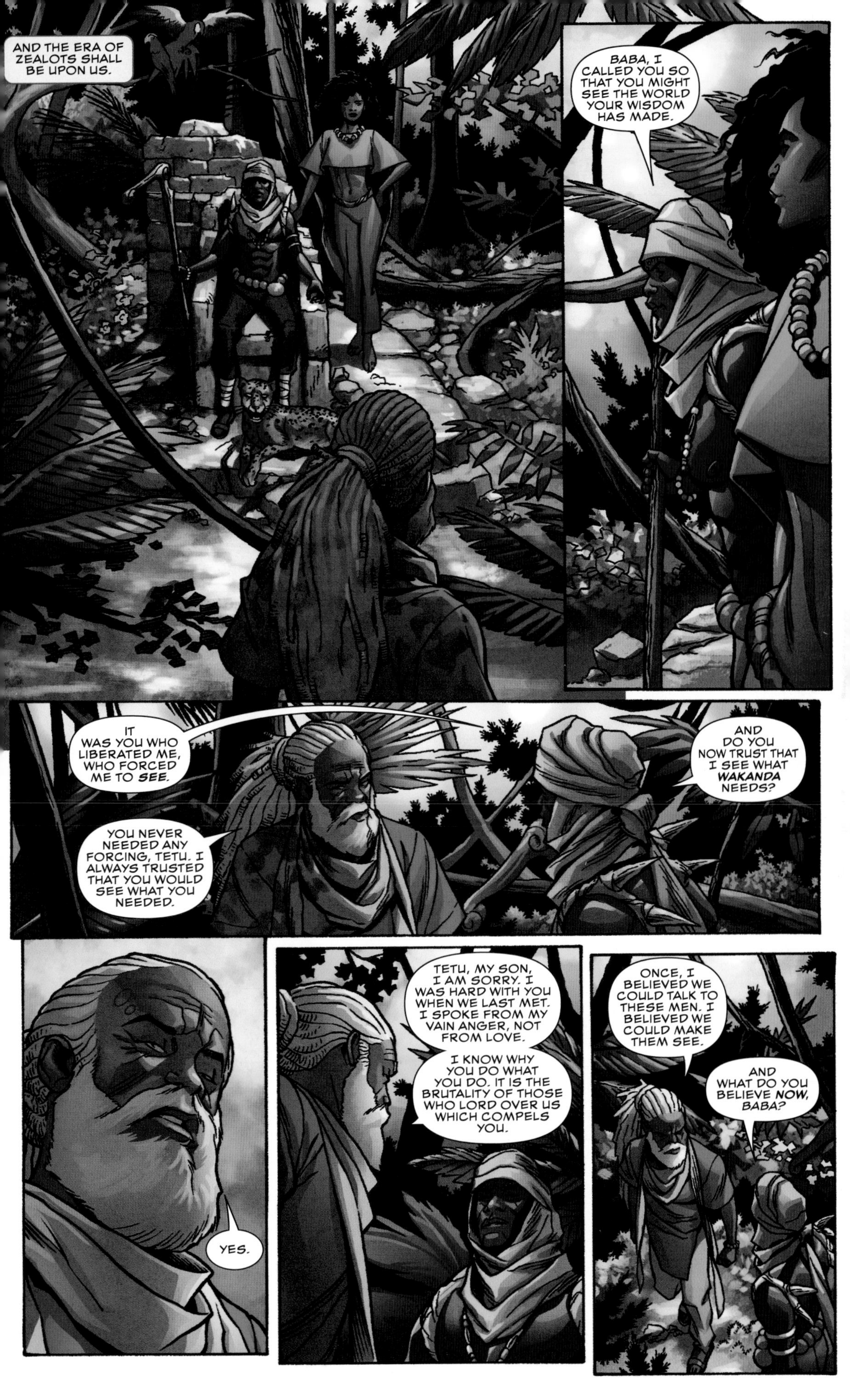

AND THE ERA OF ZEALOTS SHALL BE UPON US.
BABA, I CALLED YOU SO THAT YOU MIGHT SEE THE WORLD YOUR WISDOM HAS MADE.
IT WAS YOU WHO LIBERATED ME, WHO FORCED ME TO *SEE.*
AND DO YOU NOW TRUST THAT I SEE WHAT *WAKANDA* NEEDS?
YOU NEVER NEEDED ANY FORCING, TETU. I ALWAYS TRUSTED THAT YOU WOULD SEE WHAT YOU NEEDED.
YES.
TETU, MY SON, I AM SORRY. I WAS HARD WITH YOU WHEN WE LAST MET. I SPOKE FROM MY VAIN ANGER, NOT FROM LOVE.
I KNOW WHY YOU DO WHAT YOU DO. IT IS THE BRUTALITY OF THOSE WHO LORD OVER US WHICH COMPELS YOU.
ONCE, I BELIEVED WE COULD TALK TO THESE MEN. I BELIEVED WE COULD MAKE THEM SEE.
AND WHAT DO YOU BELIEVE *NOW,* BABA?

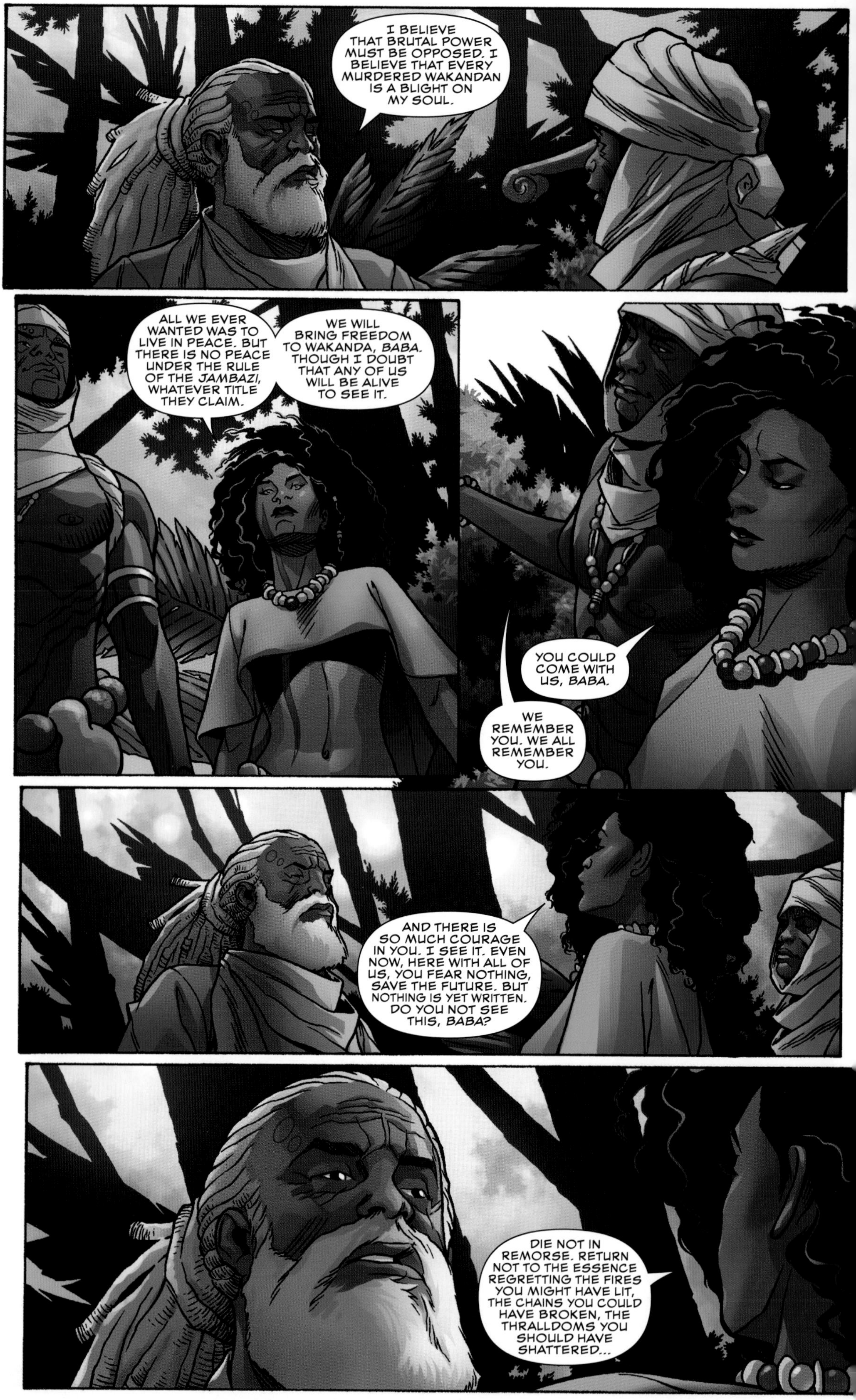
I BELIEVE THAT BRUTAL POWER MUST BE OPPOSED. I BELIEVE THAT EVERY MURDERED WAKANDAN IS A BLIGHT ON MY SOUL.
ALL WE EVER WANTED WAS TO LIVE IN PEACE. BUT THERE IS NO PEACE UNDER THE RULE OF THE *JAMBAZI*, WHATEVER TITLE THEY CLAIM.
WE WILL BRING FREEDOM TO WAKANDA, *BABA*. THOUGH I DOUBT THAT ANY OF US WILL BE ALIVE TO SEE IT.
YOU COULD COME WITH US, *BABA*.
WE REMEMBER YOU. WE ALL REMEMBER YOU.
AND THERE IS SO MUCH COURAGE IN YOU. I SEE IT. EVEN NOW, HERE WITH ALL OF US, YOU FEAR NOTHING, SAVE THE FUTURE. BUT NOTHING IS YET WRITTEN. DO YOU NOT SEE THIS, *BABA*?
DIE NOT IN REMORSE. RETURN NOT TO THE ESSENCE REGRETTING THE FIRES YOU MIGHT HAVE LIT, THE CHAINS YOU COULD HAVE BROKEN, THE THRALLDOMS YOU SHOULD HAVE SHATTERED...

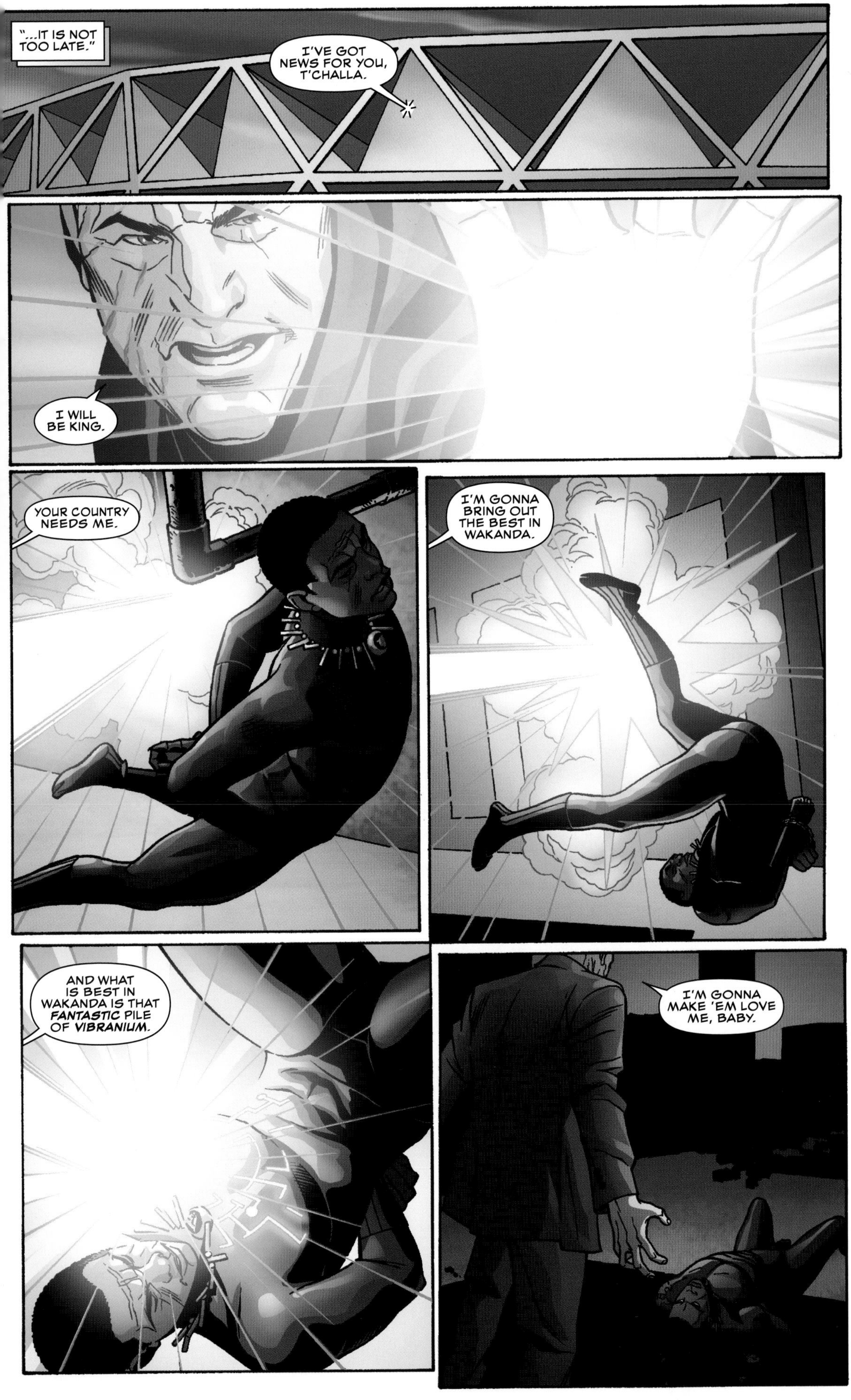
"...IT IS NOT TOO LATE."
I'VE GOT NEWS FOR YOU, T'CHALLA.
I WILL BE KING.
YOUR COUNTRY NEEDS ME.
I'M GONNA BRING OUT THE BEST IN WAKANDA.
AND WHAT IS BEST IN WAKANDA IS THAT *FANTASTIC* PILE OF **VIBRANIUM**.
I'M GONNA MAKE 'EM LOVE ME, BABY.

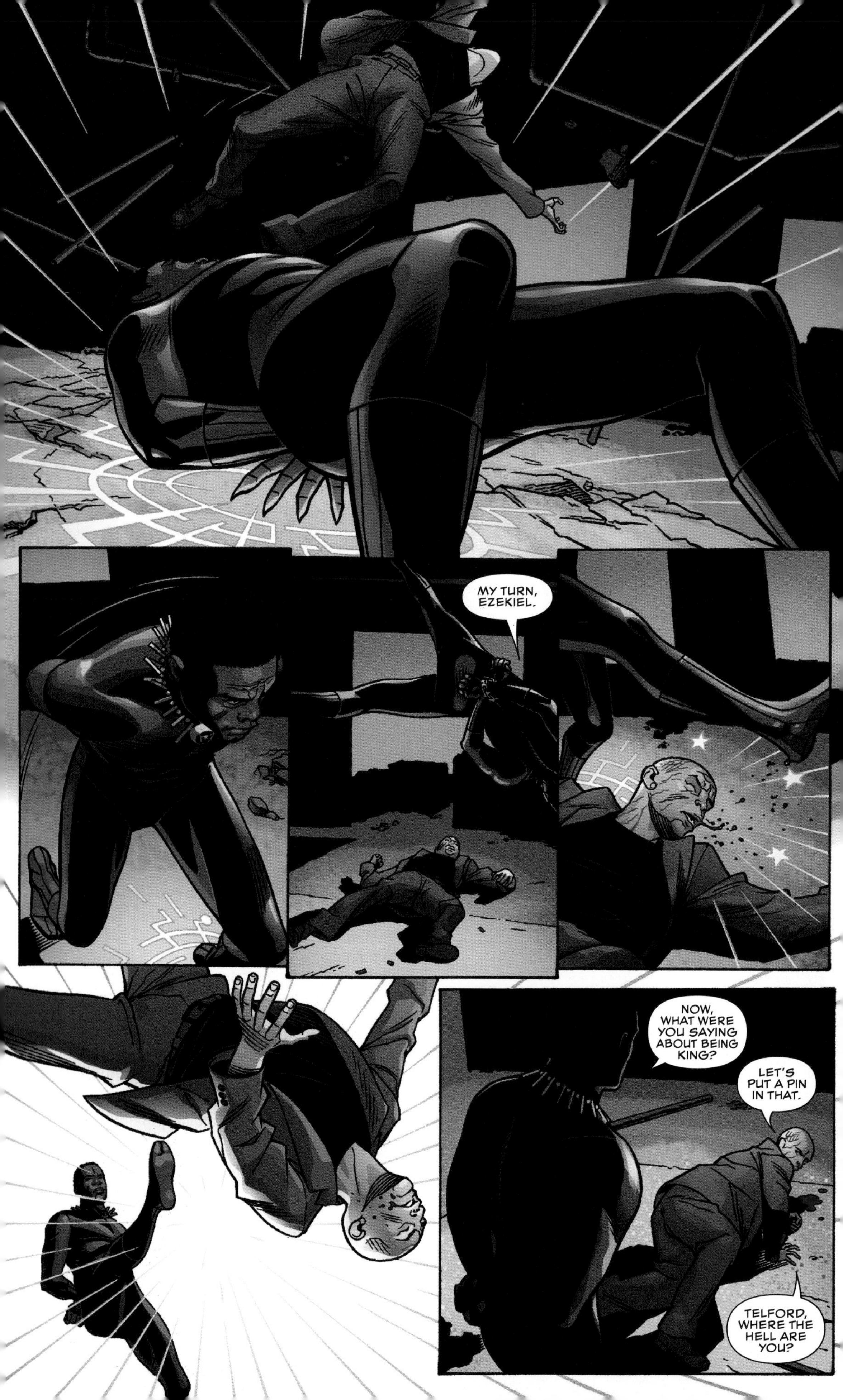
MY TURN, EZEKIEL.
NOW, WHAT WERE YOU SAYING ABOUT BEING KING?
LET'S PUT A PIN IN THAT.
TELFORD, WHERE THE HELL ARE YOU?

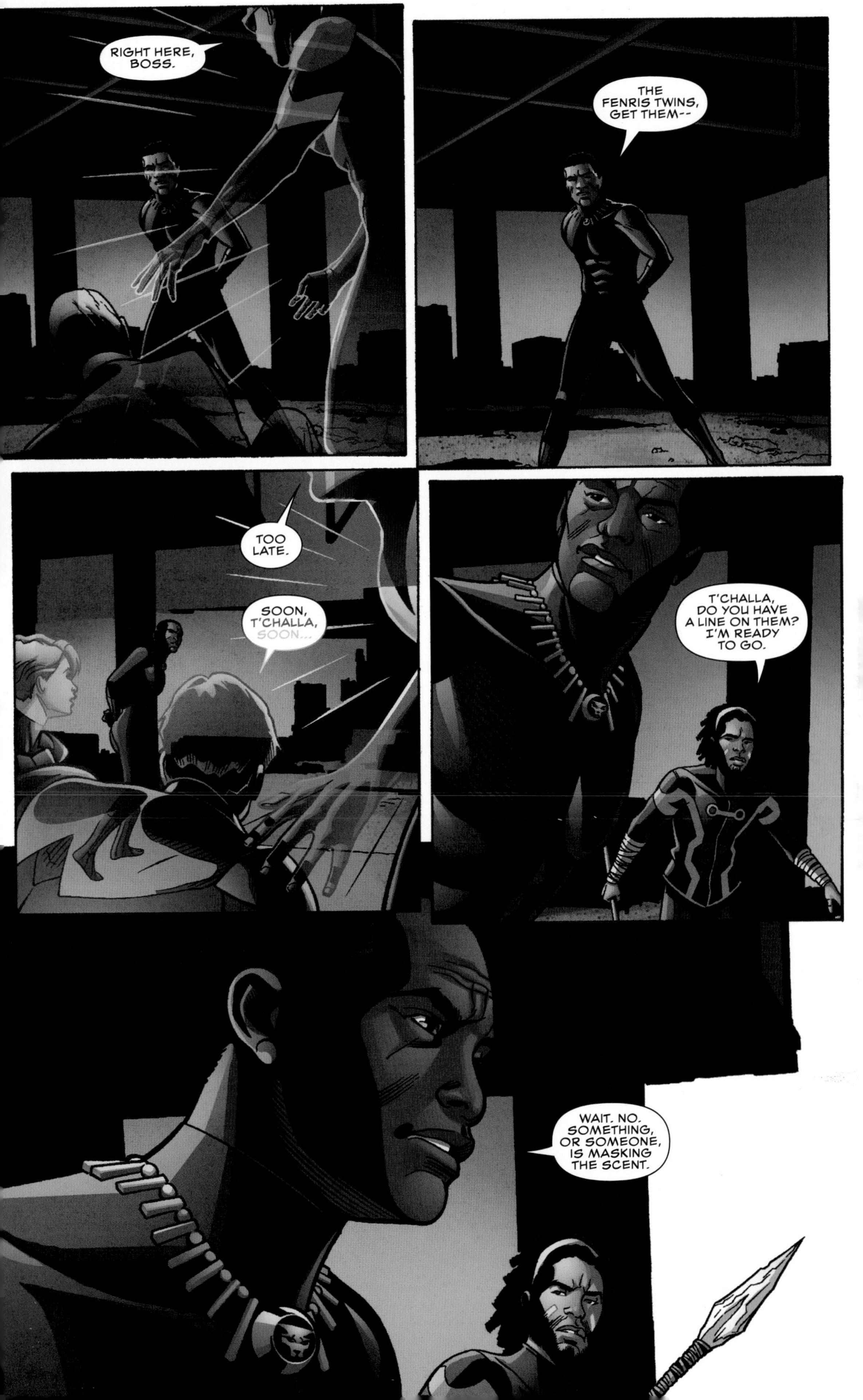
RIGHT HERE, BOSS.
THE FENRIS TWINS, GET THEM--
TOO LATE.
SOON, T'CHALLA, SOON...
T'CHALLA, DO YOU HAVE A LINE ON THEM? I'M READY TO GO.
WAIT. NO. SOMETHING, OR SOMEONE, IS MASKING THE SCENT.

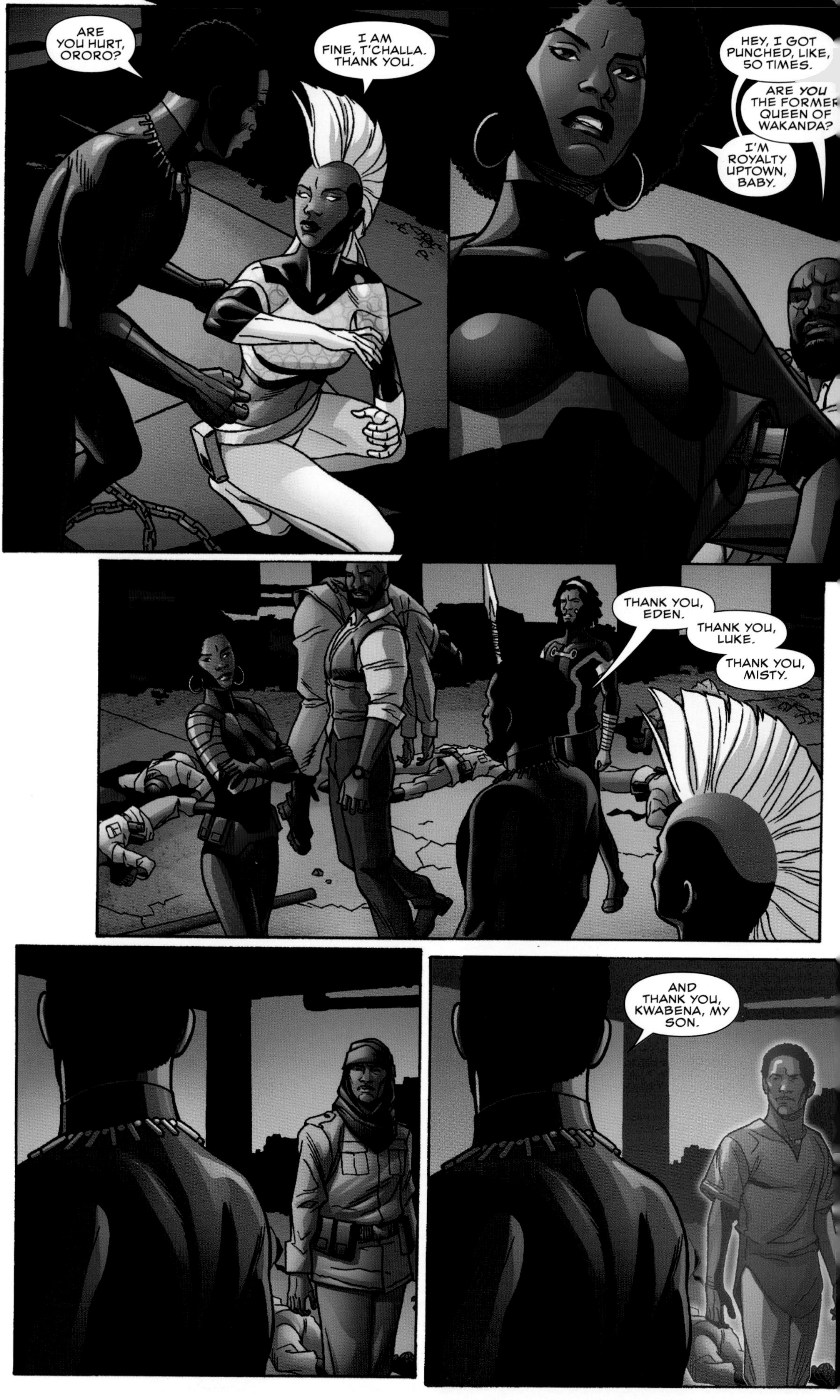

ARE YOU HURT, ORORO?
I AM FINE, T'CHALLA. THANK YOU.
HEY, I GOT PUNCHED, LIKE, 50 TIMES.
ARE YOU THE FORMER QUEEN OF WAKANDA?
I'M ROYALTY UPTOWN, BABY.
THANK YOU, EDEN.
THANK YOU, LUKE.
THANK YOU, MISTY.
AND THANK YOU, KWABENA, MY SON.

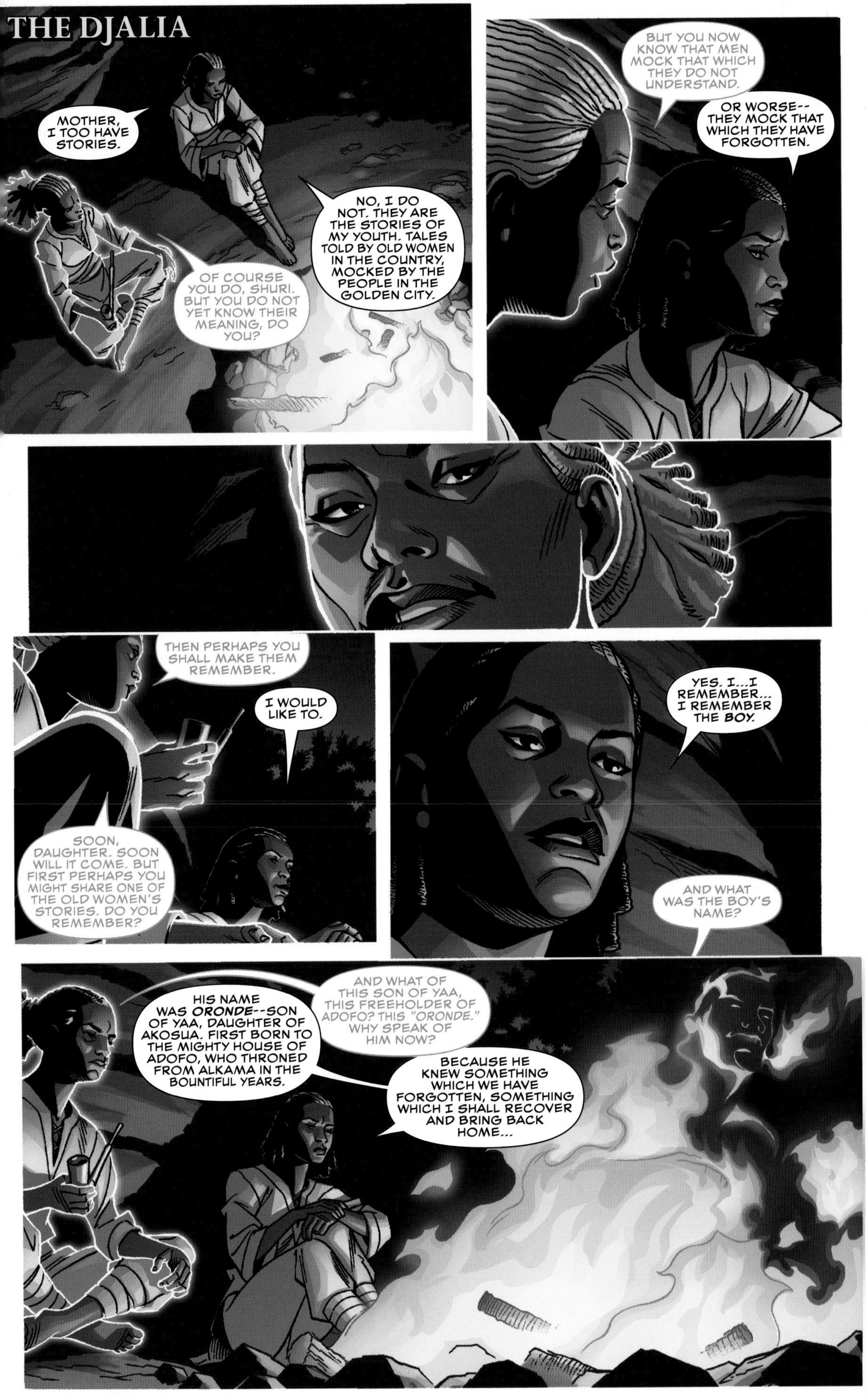
THE DJALIA
MOTHER, I TOO HAVE STORIES.
OF COURSE YOU DO, SHURI. BUT YOU DO NOT YET KNOW THEIR MEANING, DO YOU?
NO, I DO NOT. THEY ARE THE STORIES OF MY YOUTH. TALES TOLD BY OLD WOMEN IN THE COUNTRY, MOCKED BY THE PEOPLE IN THE GOLDEN CITY.
BUT YOU NOW KNOW THAT MEN MOCK THAT WHICH THEY DO NOT UNDERSTAND.
OR WORSE--THEY MOCK THAT WHICH THEY HAVE FORGOTTEN.
THEN PERHAPS YOU SHALL MAKE THEM REMEMBER.
I WOULD LIKE TO.
SOON, DAUGHTER. SOON WILL IT COME. BUT FIRST PERHAPS YOU MIGHT SHARE ONE OF THE OLD WOMEN'S STORIES. DO YOU REMEMBER?
YES. I...I REMEMBER... I REMEMBER THE BOY.
AND WHAT WAS THE BOY'S NAME?
HIS NAME WAS ORONDE--SON OF YAA, DAUGHTER OF AKOSUA. FIRST BORN TO THE MIGHTY HOUSE OF ADOFO, WHO THRONED FROM ALKAMA IN THE BOUNTIFUL YEARS.
AND WHAT OF THIS SON OF YAA, THIS FREEHOLDER OF ADOFO? THIS "ORONDE." WHY SPEAK OF HIM NOW?
BECAUSE HE KNEW SOMETHING WHICH WE HAVE FORGOTTEN, SOMETHING WHICH I SHALL RECOVER AND BRING BACK HOME...

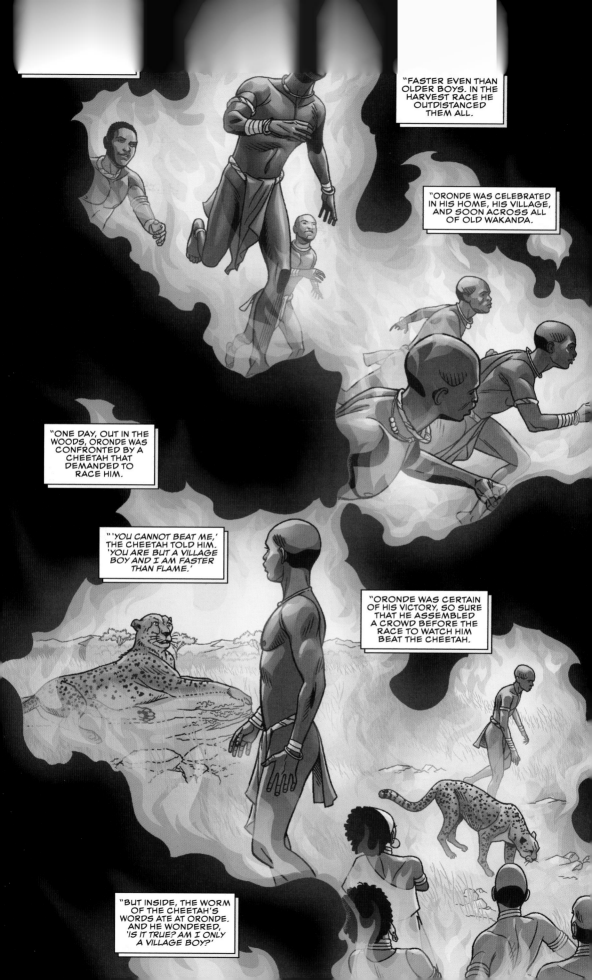

"FASTER EVEN THAN OLDER BOYS. IN THE HARVEST RACE HE OUTDISTANCED THEM ALL.

"ORONDE WAS CELEBRATED IN HIS HOME, HIS VILLAGE, AND SOON ACROSS ALL OF OLD WAKANDA.

"ONE DAY, OUT IN THE WOODS, ORONDE WAS CONFRONTED BY A CHEETAH THAT DEMANDED TO RACE HIM.

"'YOU CANNOT BEAT ME,' THE CHEETAH TOLD HIM. 'YOU ARE BUT A VILLAGE BOY AND I AM FASTER THAN FLAME.'

"ORONDE WAS CERTAIN OF HIS VICTORY, SO SURE THAT HE ASSEMBLED A CROWD BEFORE THE RACE TO WATCH HIM BEAT THE CHEETAH.

"BUT INSIDE, THE WORM OF THE CHEETAH'S WORDS ATE AT ORONDE. AND HE WONDERED, 'IS IT TRUE? AM I ONLY A VILLAGE BOY?'

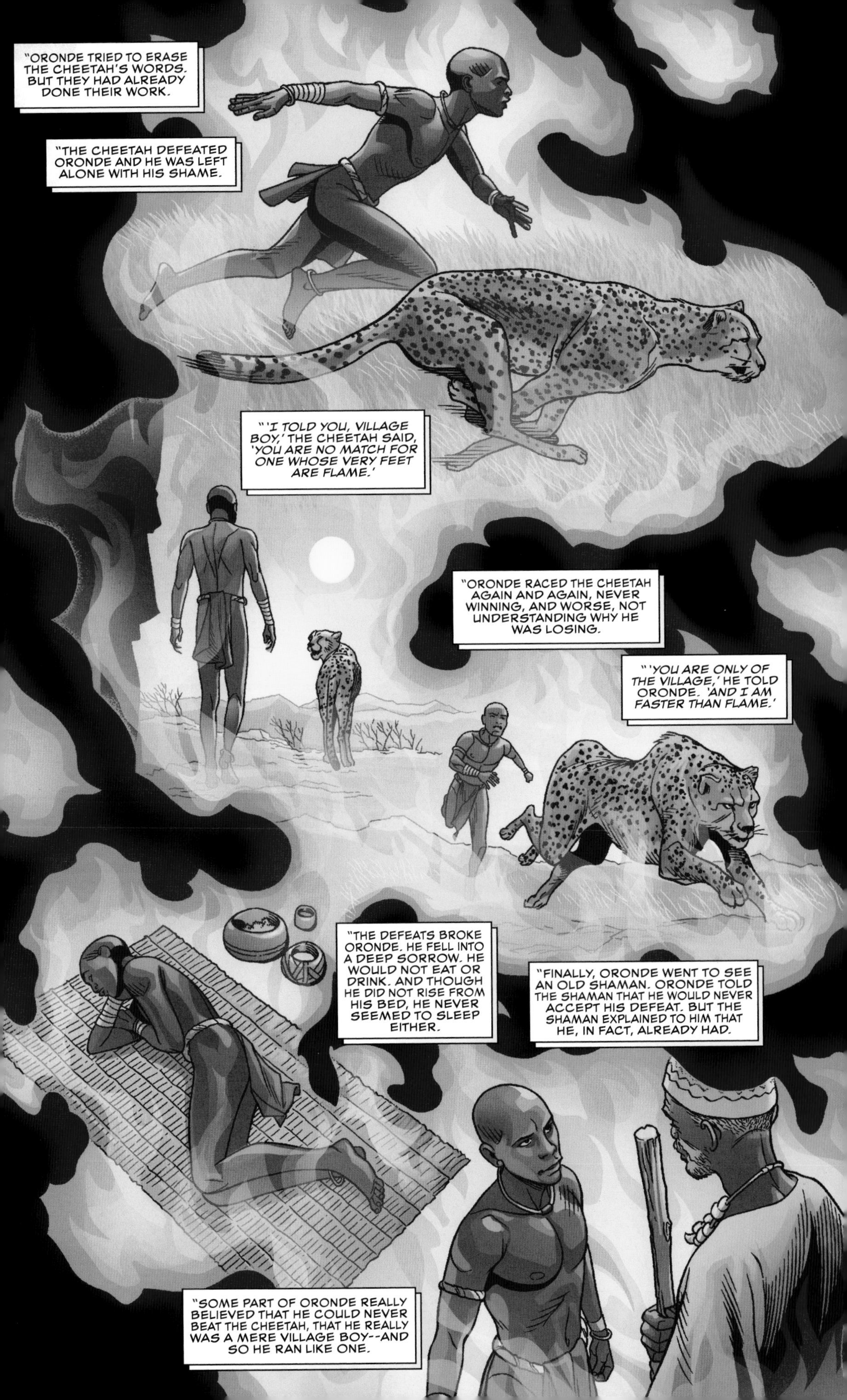
"ORONDE TRIED TO ERASE THE CHEETAH'S WORDS. BUT THEY HAD ALREADY DONE THEIR WORK.
"THE CHEETAH DEFEATED ORONDE AND HE WAS LEFT ALONE WITH HIS SHAME.
"'I TOLD YOU, VILLAGE BOY,' THE CHEETAH SAID, 'YOU ARE NO MATCH FOR ONE WHOSE VERY FEET ARE FLAME.'
"ORONDE RACED THE CHEETAH AGAIN AND AGAIN, NEVER WINNING, AND WORSE, NOT UNDERSTANDING WHY HE WAS LOSING.
"'YOU ARE ONLY OF THE VILLAGE,' HE TOLD ORONDE. 'AND I AM FASTER THAN FLAME.'
"THE DEFEATS BROKE ORONDE. HE FELL INTO A DEEP SORROW. HE WOULD NOT EAT OR DRINK. AND THOUGH HE DID NOT RISE FROM HIS BED, HE NEVER SEEMED TO SLEEP EITHER.
"FINALLY, ORONDE WENT TO SEE AN OLD SHAMAN. ORONDE TOLD THE SHAMAN THAT HE WOULD NEVER ACCEPT HIS DEFEAT. BUT THE SHAMAN EXPLAINED TO HIM THAT HE, IN FACT, ALREADY HAD.
"SOME PART OF ORONDE REALLY BELIEVED THAT HE COULD NEVER BEAT THE CHEETAH, THAT HE REALLY WAS A MERE VILLAGE BOY--AND SO HE RAN LIKE ONE.

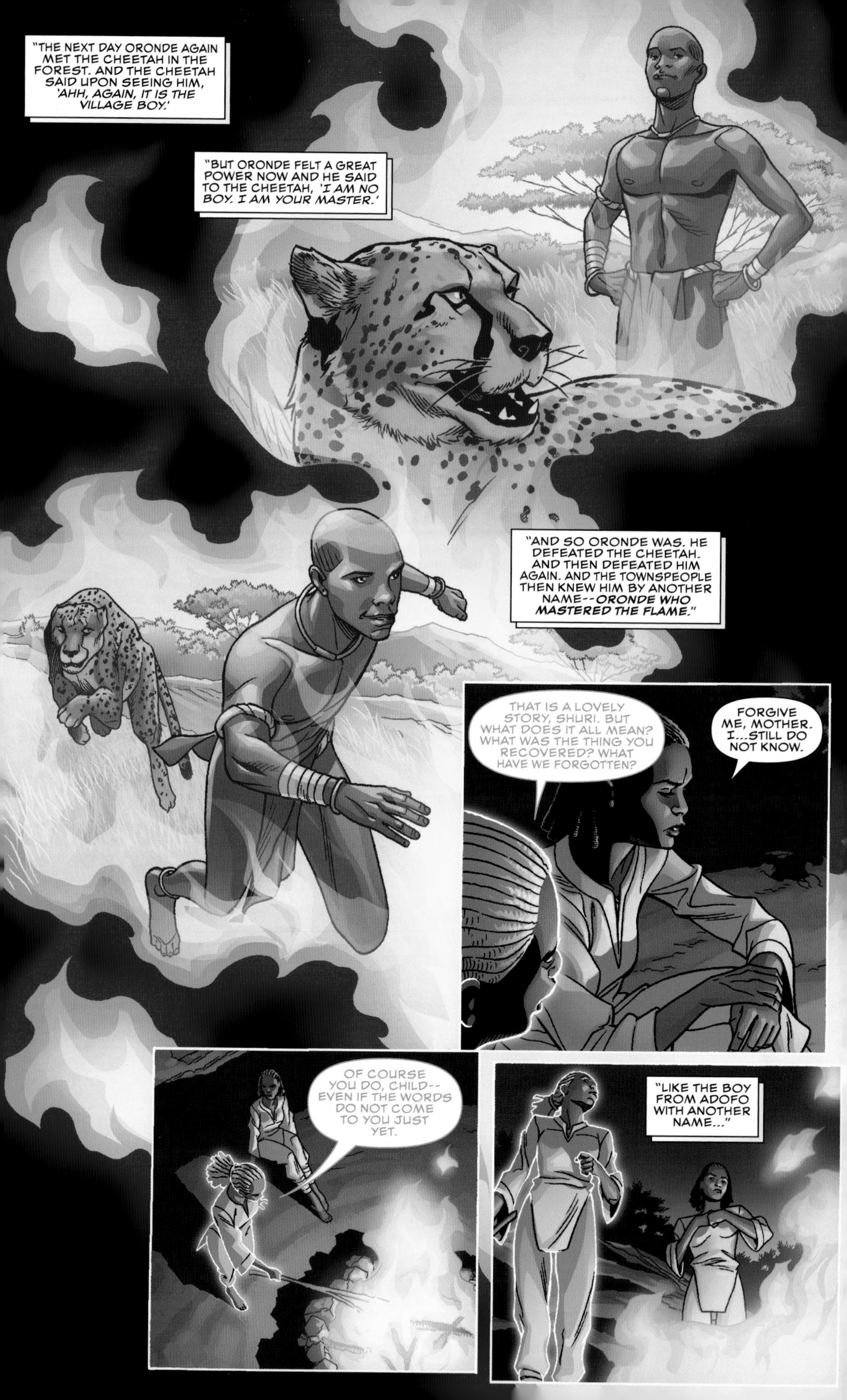
"THE NEXT DAY ORONDE AGAIN MET THE CHEETAH IN THE FOREST. AND THE CHEETAH SAID UPON SEEING HIM, 'AHH, AGAIN, IT IS THE VILLAGE BOY.'
"BUT ORONDE FELT A GREAT POWER NOW AND HE SAID TO THE CHEETAH, 'I AM NO BOY. I AM YOUR MASTER.'
"AND SO ORONDE WAS. HE DEFEATED THE CHEETAH. AND THEN DEFEATED HIM AGAIN. AND THE TOWNSPEOPLE THEN KNEW HIM BY ANOTHER NAME--ORONDE WHO MASTERED THE FLAME."
THAT IS A LOVELY STORY, SHURI. BUT WHAT DOES IT ALL MEAN? WHAT WAS THE THING YOU RECOVERED? WHAT HAVE WE FORGOTTEN?
FORGIVE ME, MOTHER. I...STILL DO NOT KNOW.
OF COURSE YOU DO, CHILD--EVEN IF THE WORDS DO NOT COME TO YOU JUST YET.
"LIKE THE BOY FROM ADOFO WITH ANOTHER NAME..."

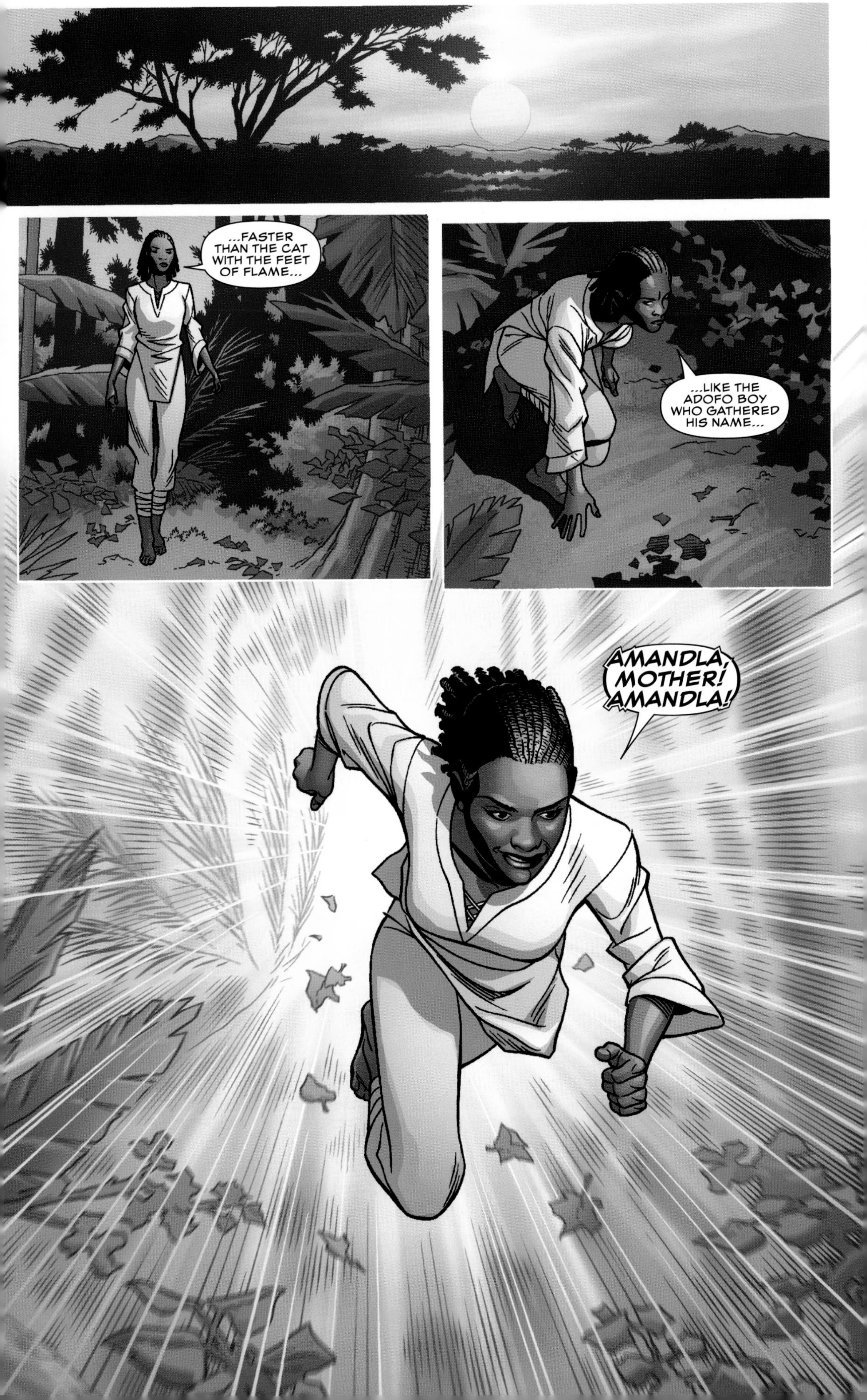
...FASTER THAN THE CAT WITH THE FEET OF FLAME...
...LIKE THE ADOFO BOY WHO GATHERED HIS NAME...
AMANDLA, MOTHER! AMANDLA!

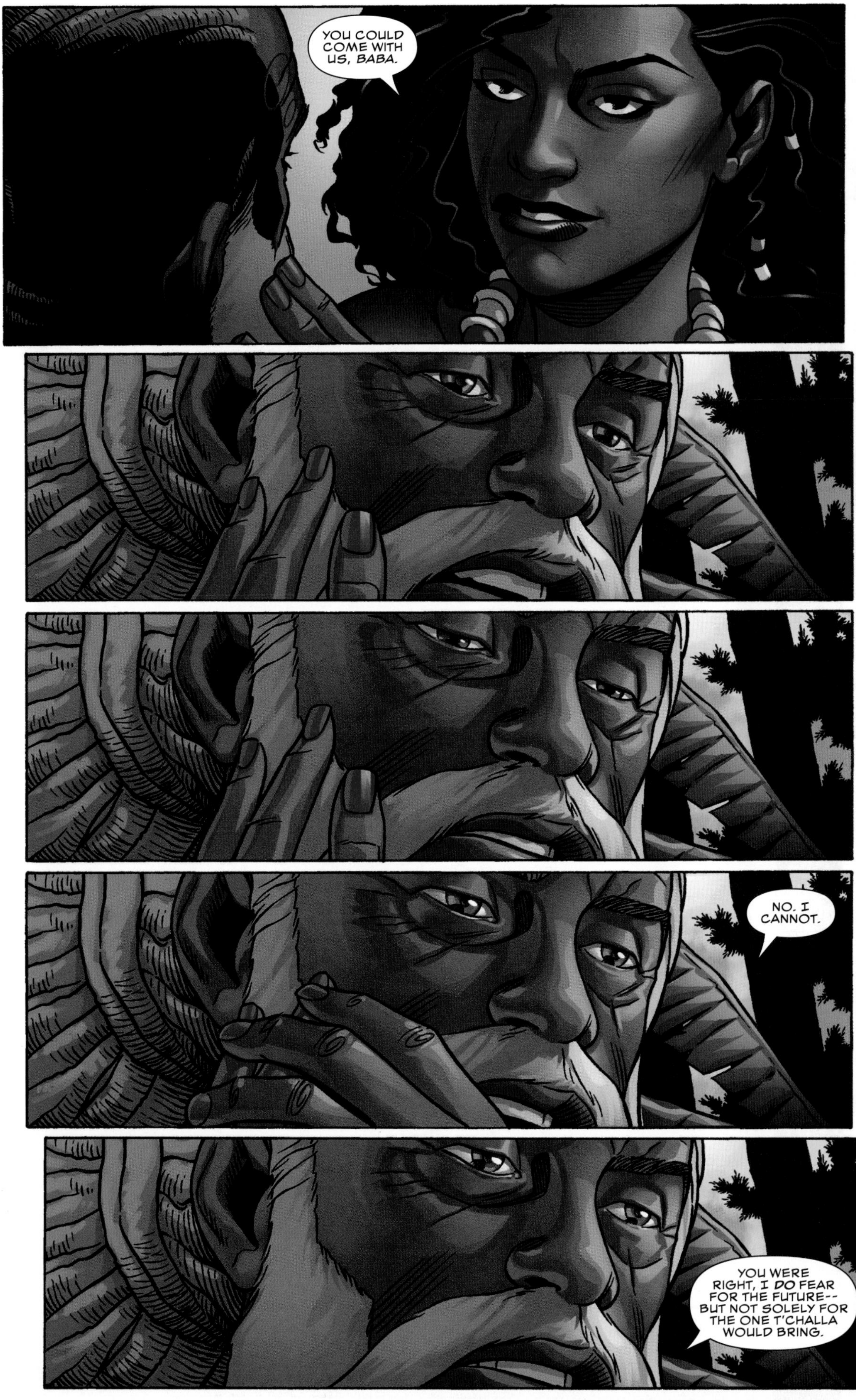
YOU COULD COME WITH US, *BABA.*
NO. I CANNOT.
YOU WERE RIGHT, I *DO* FEAR FOR THE FUTURE-- BUT NOT SOLELY FOR THE ONE T'CHALLA WOULD BRING.

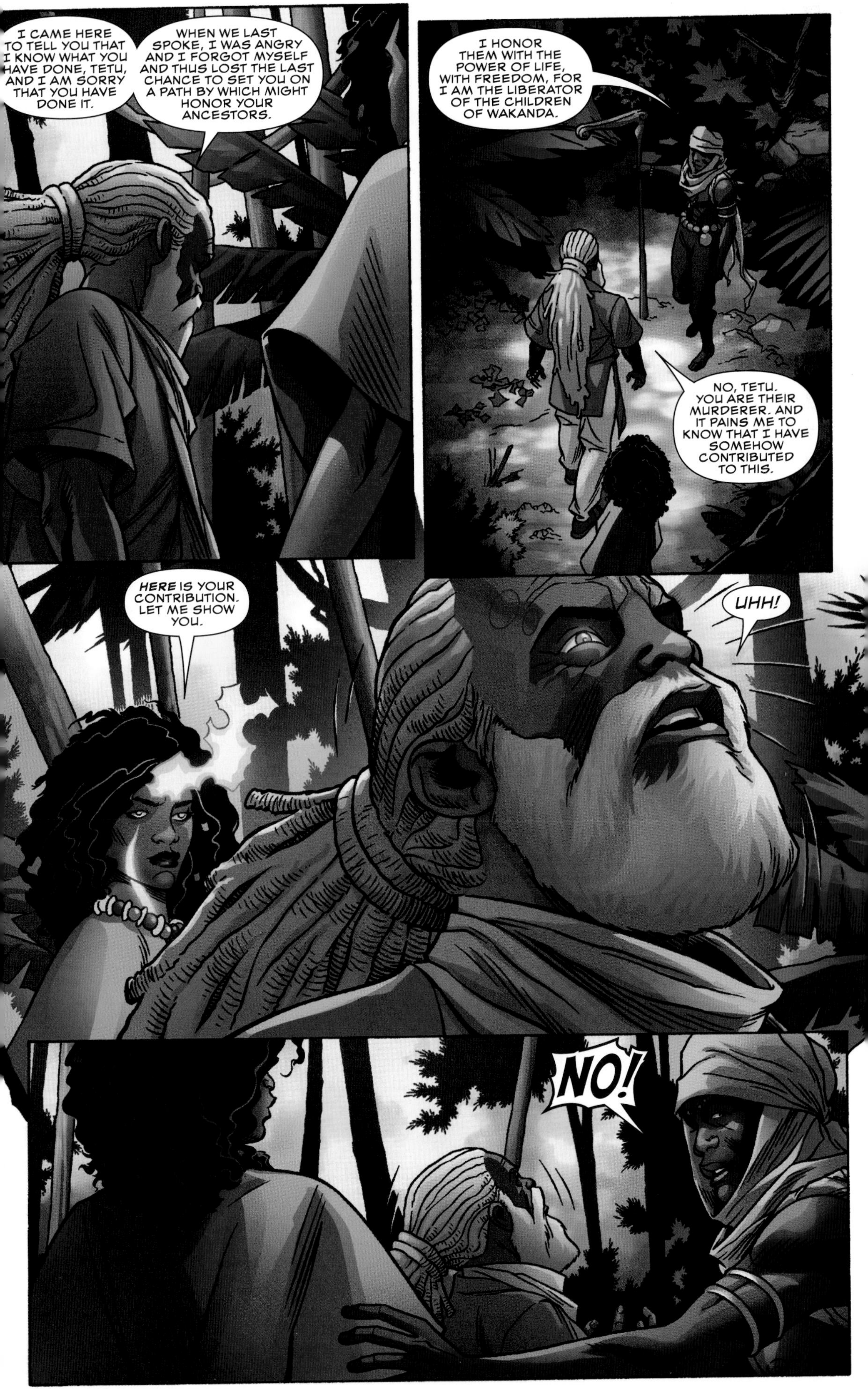
I CAME HERE TO TELL YOU THAT I KNOW WHAT YOU HAVE DONE, TETU, AND I AM SORRY THAT YOU HAVE DONE IT.
WHEN WE LAST SPOKE, I WAS ANGRY AND I FORGOT MYSELF AND THUS LOST THE LAST CHANCE TO SET YOU ON A PATH BY WHICH MIGHT HONOR YOUR ANCESTORS.
I HONOR THEM WITH THE POWER OF LIFE, WITH FREEDOM, FOR I AM THE LIBERATOR OF THE CHILDREN OF WAKANDA.
NO, TETU. YOU ARE THEIR MURDERER. AND IT PAINS ME TO KNOW THAT I HAVE SOMEHOW CONTRIBUTED TO THIS.
HERE IS YOUR CONTRIBUTION. LET ME SHOW YOU.
UHH!
NO!

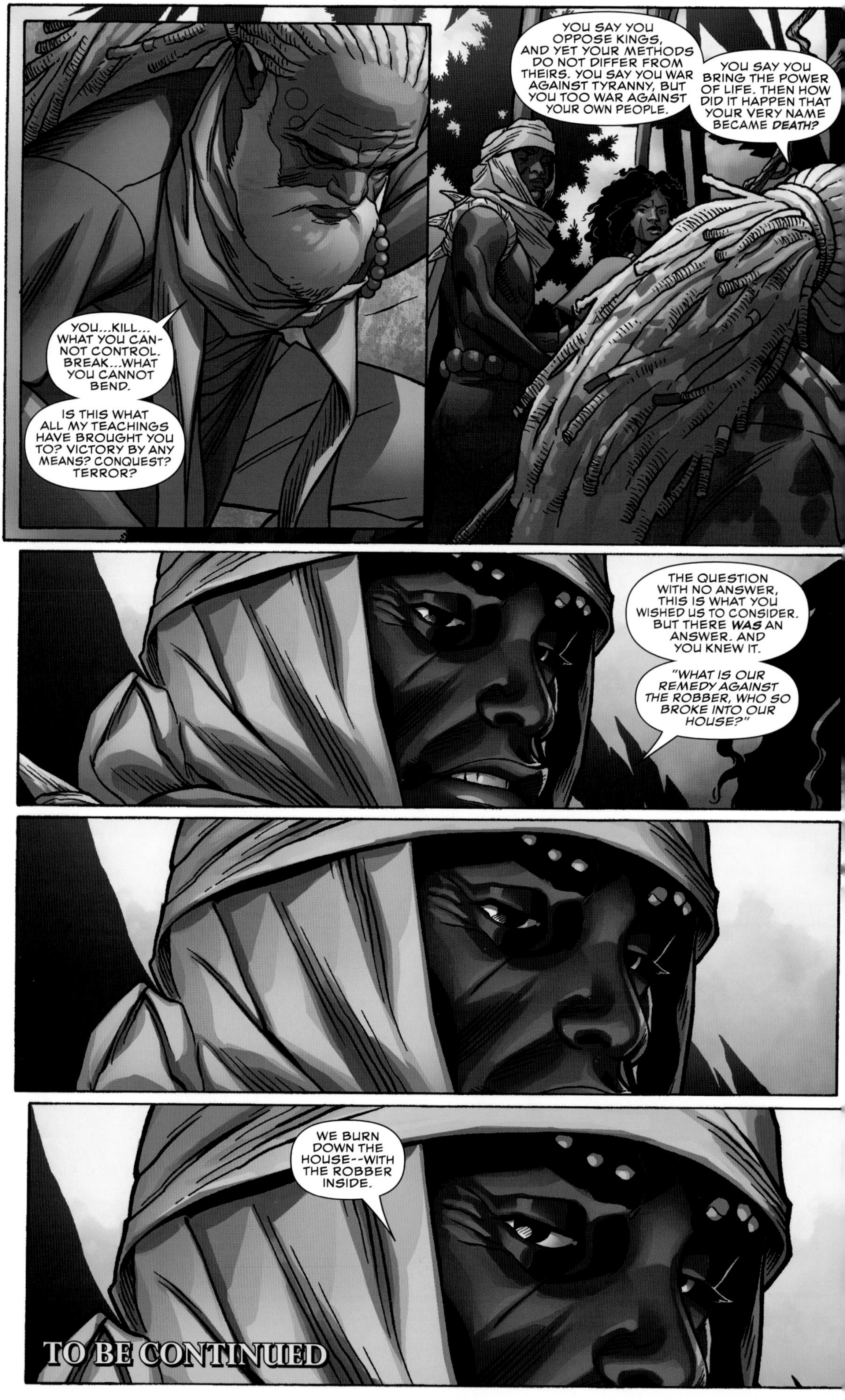
YOU...KILL... WHAT YOU CAN-NOT CONTROL. BREAK...WHAT YOU CANNOT BEND.
IS THIS WHAT ALL MY TEACHINGS HAVE BROUGHT YOU TO? VICTORY BY ANY MEANS? CONQUEST? TERROR?
YOU SAY YOU OPPOSE KINGS, AND YET YOUR METHODS DO NOT DIFFER FROM THEIRS. YOU SAY YOU WAR AGAINST TYRANNY, BUT YOU TOO WAR AGAINST YOUR OWN PEOPLE.
YOU SAY YOU BRING THE POWER OF LIFE. THEN HOW DID IT HAPPEN THAT YOUR VERY NAME BECAME *DEATH?*
THE QUESTION WITH NO ANSWER, THIS IS WHAT YOU WISHED US TO CONSIDER. BUT THERE *WAS* AN ANSWER. AND YOU KNEW IT.
"WHAT IS OUR REMEDY AGAINST THE ROBBER, WHO SO BROKE INTO OUR HOUSE?"
WE BURN DOWN THE HOUSE--WITH THE ROBBER INSIDE.
TO BE CONTINUED